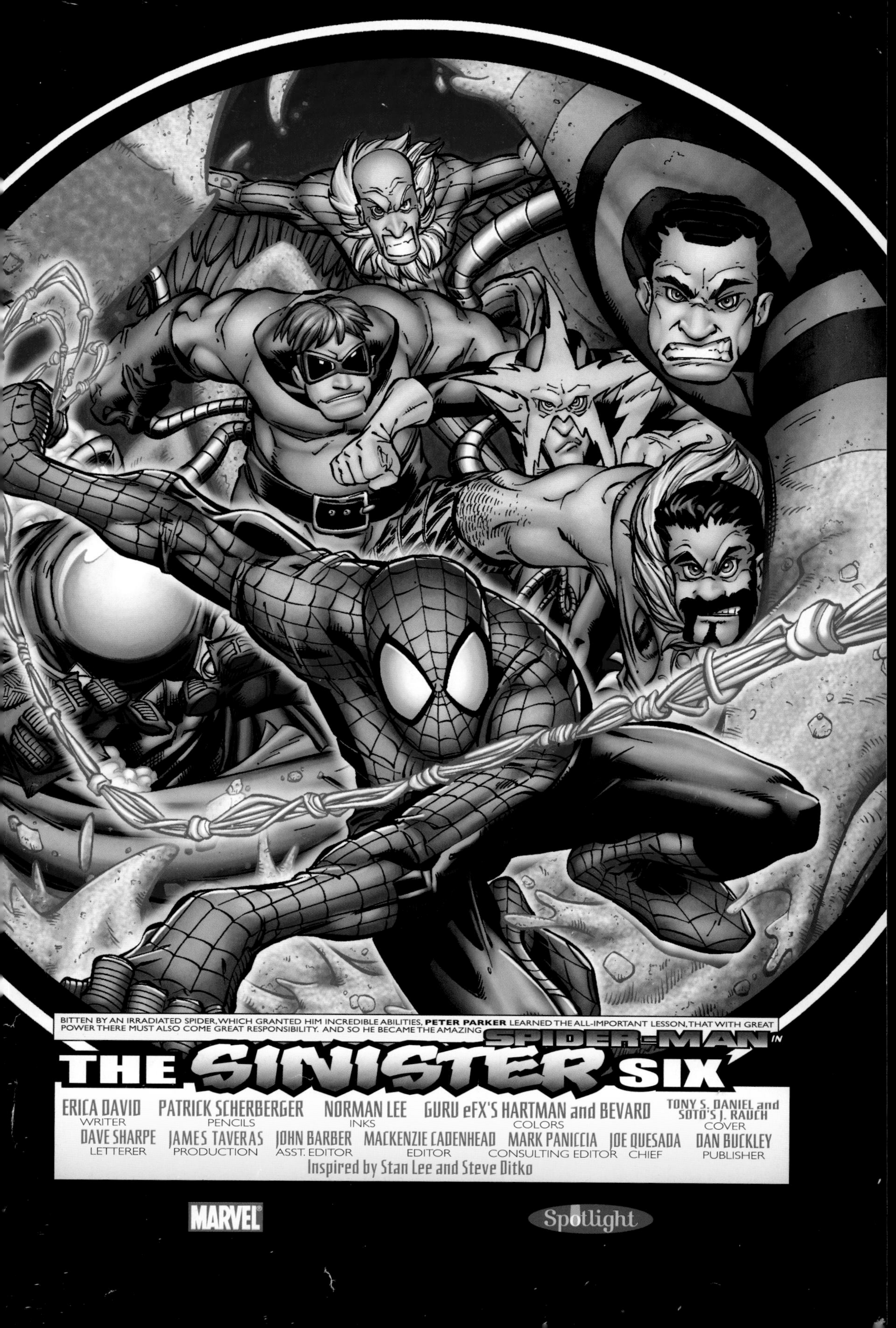

BITTEN BY AN IRRADIATED SPIDER, WHICH GRANTED HIM INCREDIBLE ABILITIES, **PETER PARKER** LEARNED THE ALL-IMPORTANT LESSON, THAT WITH GREAT POWER THERE MUST ALSO COME GREAT RESPONSIBILITY. AND SO HE BECAME THE AMAZING SPIDER-MAN IN

THE SINISTER SIX

ERICA DAVID — WRITER
PATRICK SCHERBERGER — PENCILS
NORMAN LEE — INKS
GURU eFX'S HARTMAN and BEVARD — COLORS
TONY S. DANIEL and SOTO'S J. RAUCH — COVER
DAVE SHARPE — LETTERER
JAMES TAVERAS — PRODUCTION
JOHN BARBER — ASST. EDITOR
MACKENZIE CADENHEAD — EDITOR
MARK PANICCIA — CONSULTING EDITOR
JOE QUESADA — CHIEF
DAN BUCKLEY — PUBLISHER

Inspired by Stan Lee and Steve Ditko

MARVEL

Spotlight

VISIT US AT
www.abdopublishing.com

Spotlight library bound edition © 2007. Spotlight is a division of ABDO Publishing Company, Edina, Minnesota.

Cataloging Data

David, Erica
    The sinister six / Erica David, writer ; Patrick Scherberger, pencils ; Norman Lee, inks. -- Library bound ed.
        p. cm. -- (Spider-Man)
    Summary: Introduces readers of all ages to some of the greatest stories of the legendary Marvel Universe.
    "Marvel age"--Cover.
    Revision of the July 2005 issue of the Marvel adventures Spider-Man.
    ISBN-13: 978-1-59961-216-4 (Reinforced Library Bound Edition)
    ISBN-10: 1-59961-216-X (Reinforced Library Bound Edition)
    1. Spider-Man (Fictitious character)--Fiction. 2. Comic books, strips, etc.-- Fiction. 3. Graphic novels. I. Title. II. Series.

741.5dc22

All Spotlight books are reinforced library binding and manufactured in the United States of America

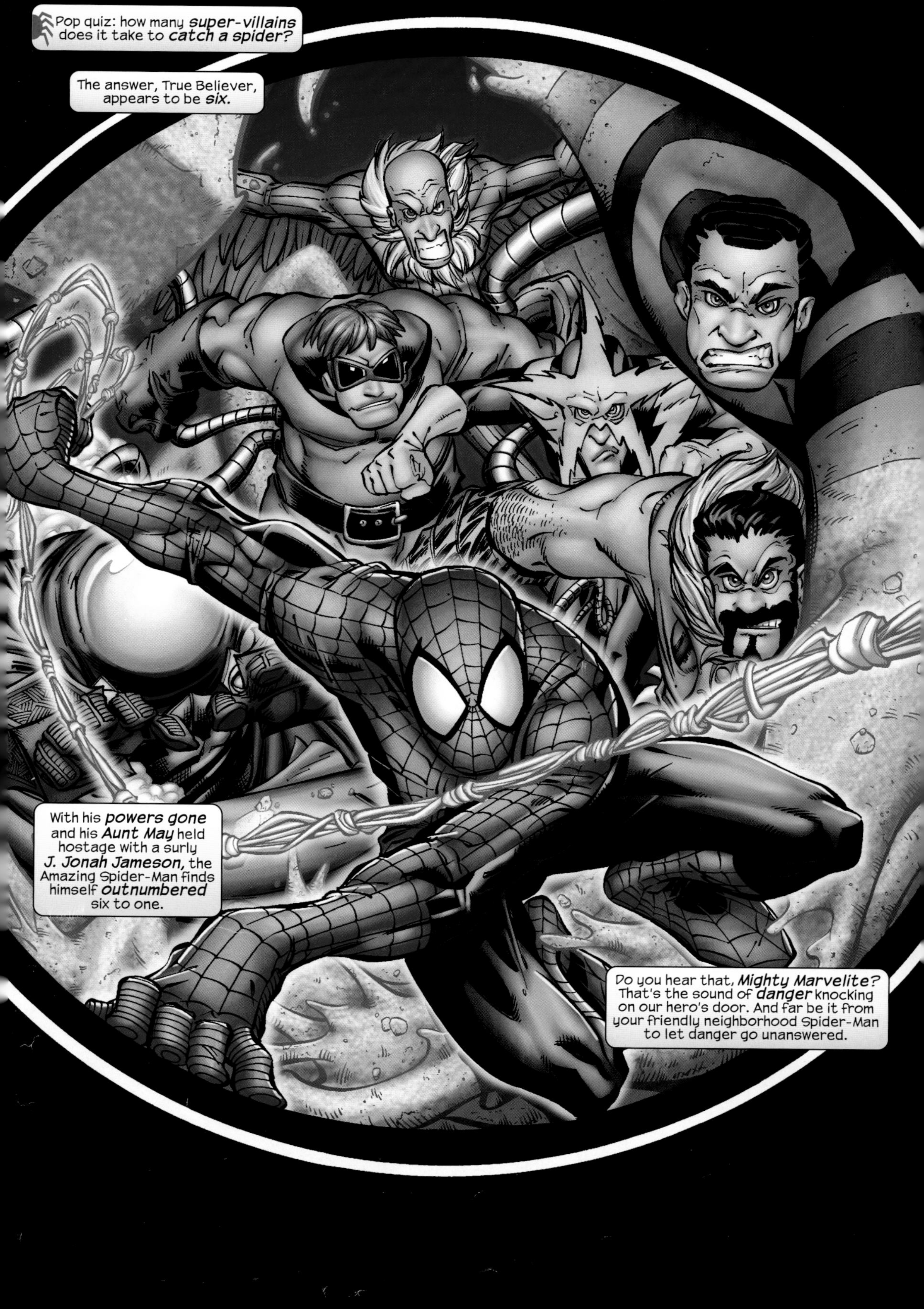

Pop quiz: how many super-villains does it take to catch a spider?
The answer, True Believer, appears to be six.
With his powers gone and his Aunt May held hostage with a surly J. Jonah Jameson, the Amazing Spider-Man finds himself outnumbered six to one.
Do you hear that, Mighty Marvelite? That's the sound of danger knocking on our hero's door. And far be it from your friendly neighborhood Spider-Man to let danger go unanswered.

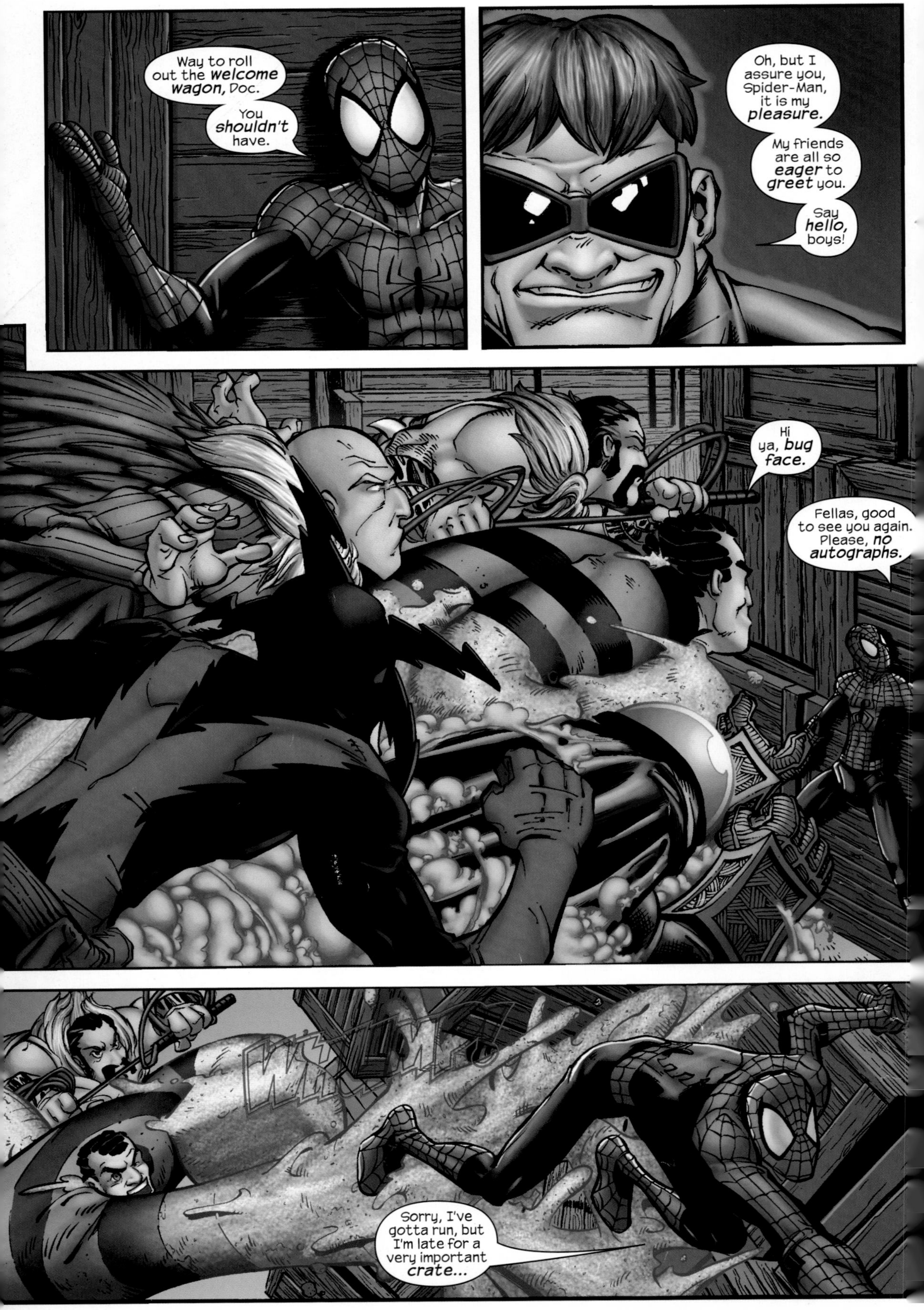
Way to roll out the *welcome wagon,* Doc.
You *shouldn't* have.
Oh, but I assure you, Spider-Man, it is my *pleasure.*
My friends are all so *eager* to *greet* you.
Say *hello,* boys!
Hi ya, *bug face.*
Fellas, good to see you again. Please, *no autographs.*
Sorry, I've gotta run, but I'm late for a very important *crate...*

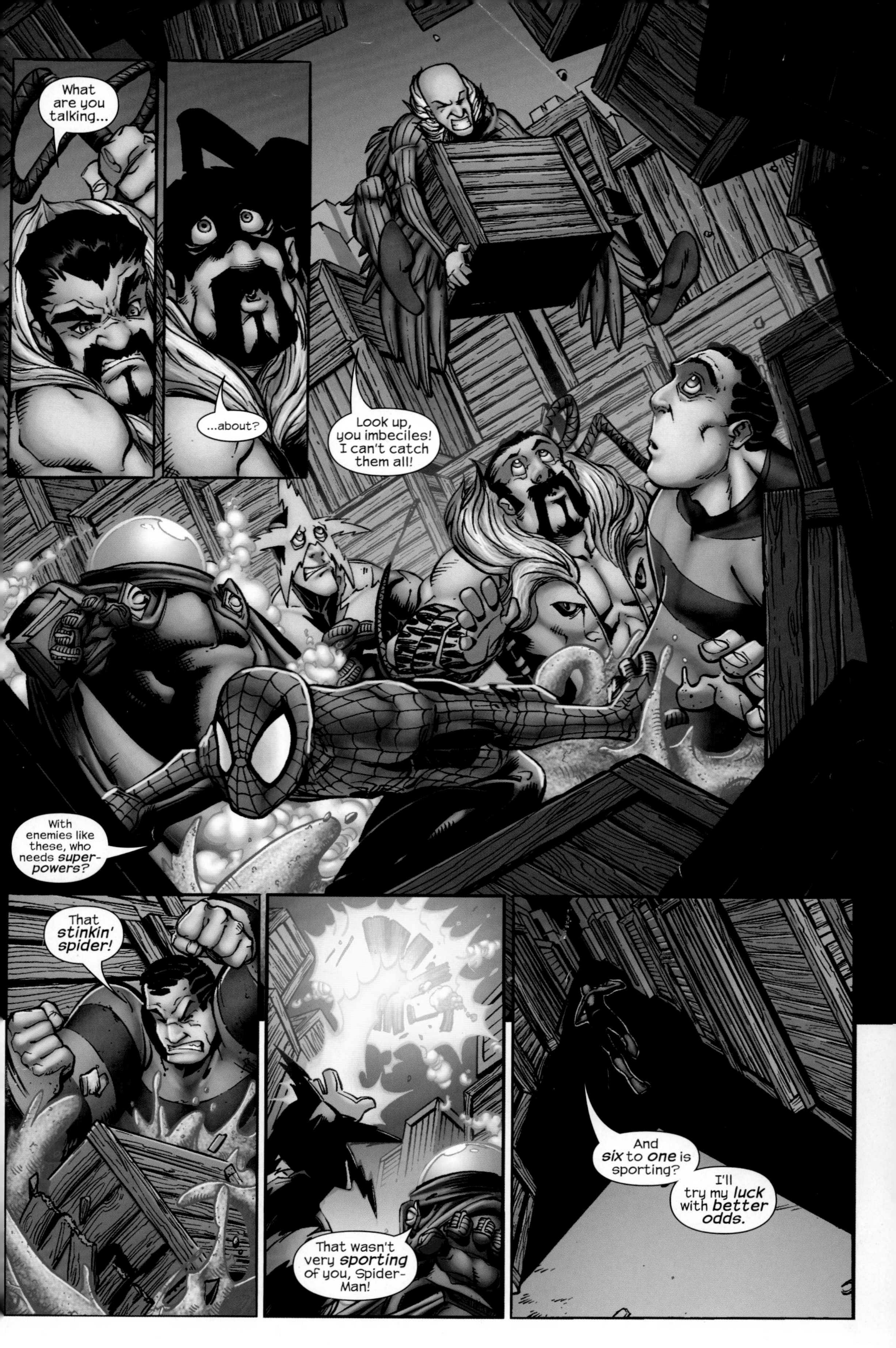
What are you talking...
...about?
Look up, you imbeciles! I can't catch them all!
With enemies like these, who needs *super-powers*?
That *stinkin' spider!*
That wasn't very *sporting* of you, Spider-Man!
And *six* to *one* is sporting?
I'll try my *luck* with *better odds.*

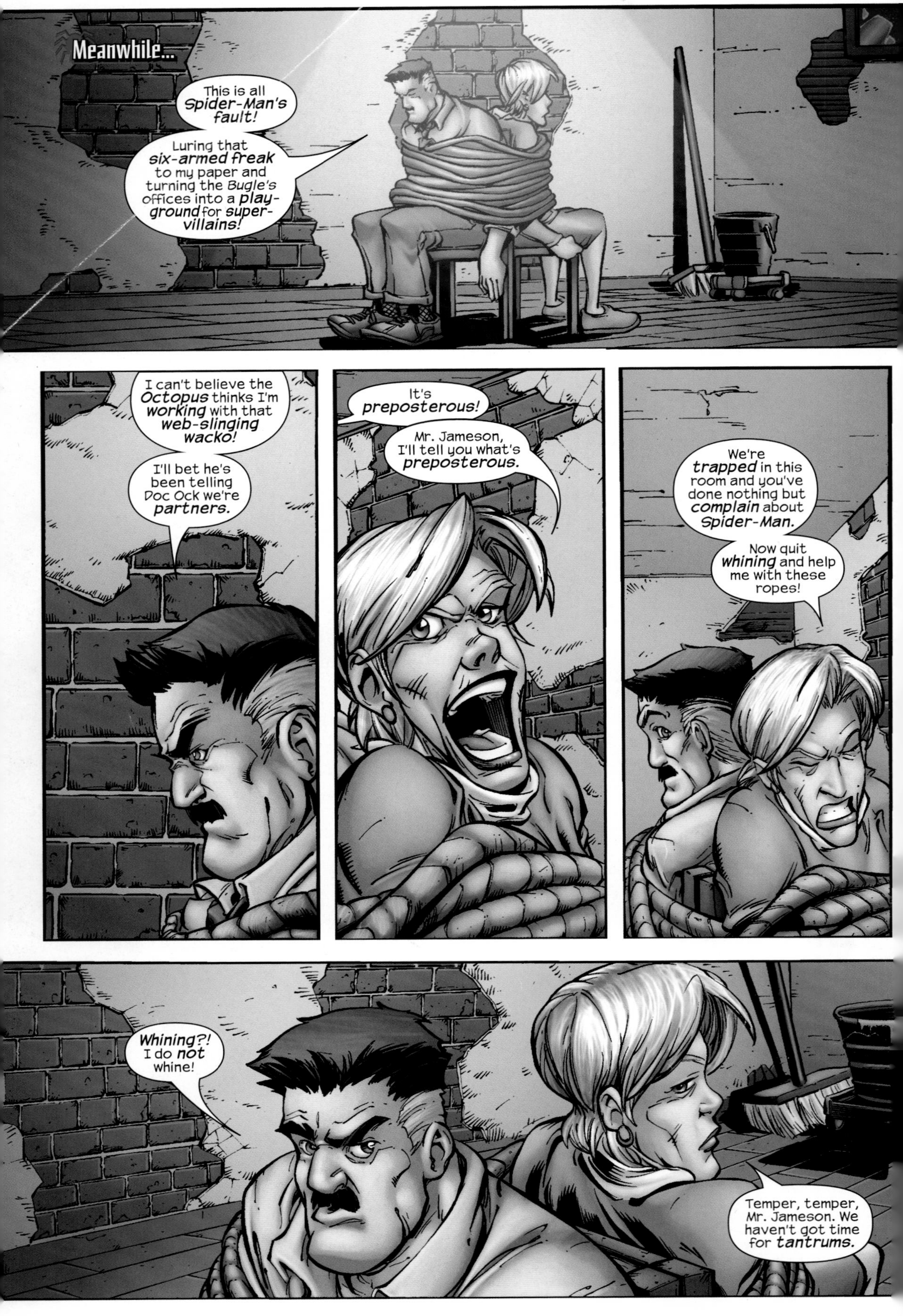
Meanwhile...
This is all Spider-Man's fault!
Luring that six-armed freak to my paper and turning the Bugle's offices into a playground for super-villains!
I can't believe the Octopus thinks I'm working with that web-slinging wacko!
I'll bet he's been telling Doc Ock we're partners.
It's preposterous!
Mr. Jameson, I'll tell you what's preposterous.
We're trapped in this room and you've done nothing but complain about Spider-Man.
Now quit whining and help me with these ropes!
Whining?! I do not whine!
Temper, temper, Mr. Jameson. We haven't got time for tantrums.

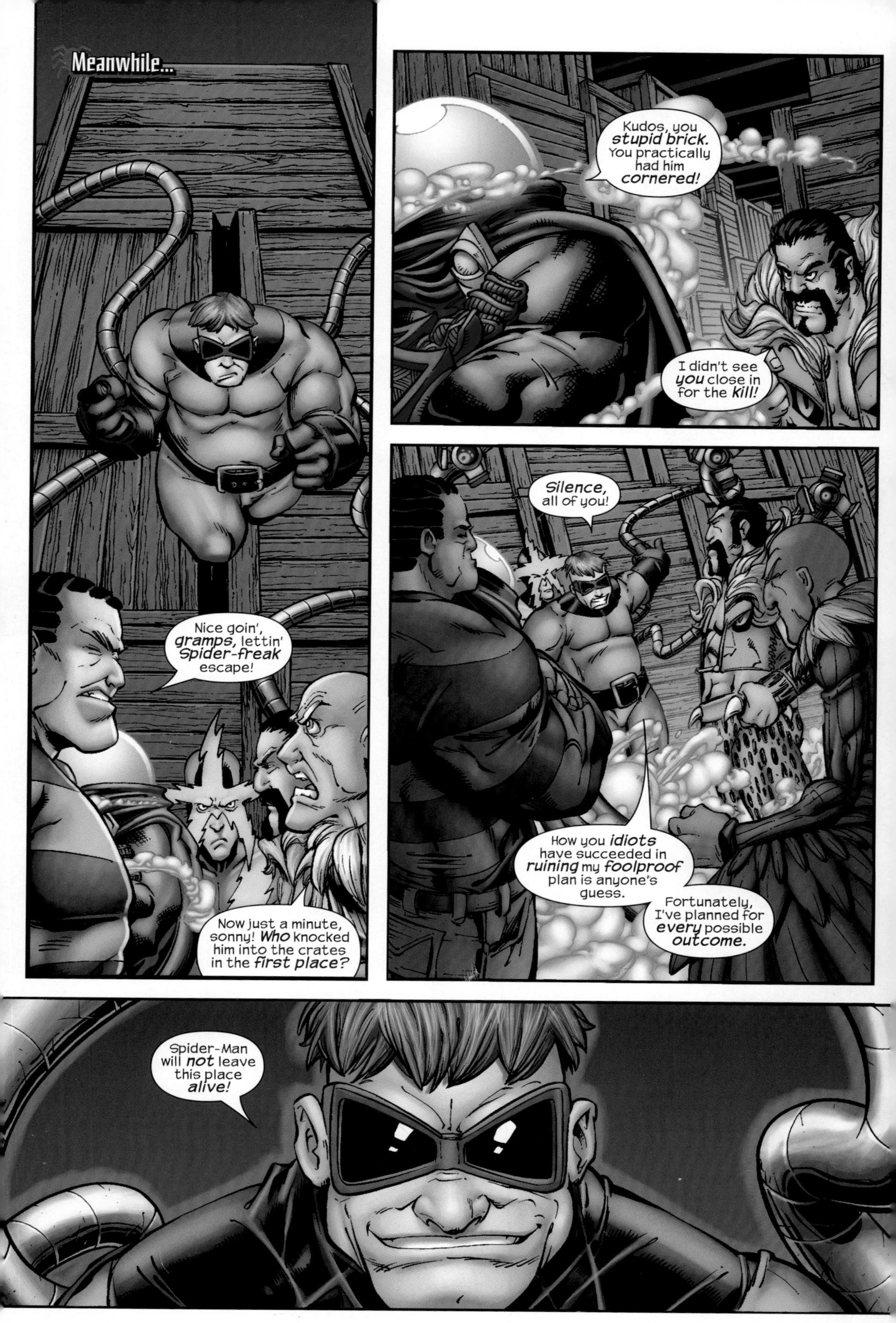
Meanwhile...
Nice goin', gramps, lettin' Spider-freak escape!
Now just a minute, sonny! Who knocked him into the crates in the first place?
Kudos, you stupid brick. You practically had him cornered!
I didn't see you close in for the kill!
Silence, all of you!
How you idiots have succeeded in ruining my foolproof plan is anyone's guess.
Fortunately, I've planned for every possible outcome.
Spider-Man will not leave this place alive!

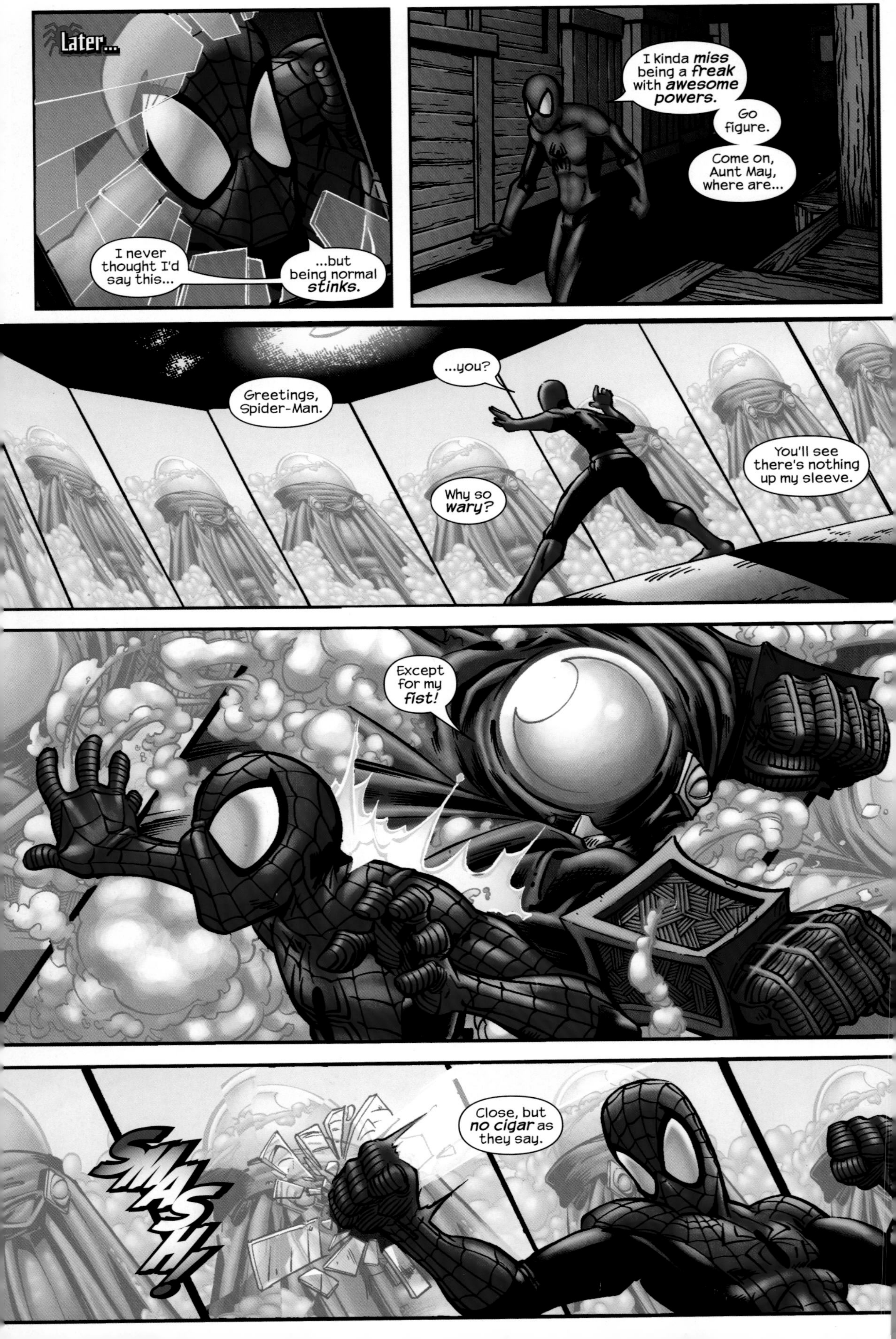
Later...
I never thought I'd say this...
...but being normal stinks.
I kinda miss being a freak with awesome powers.
Go figure.
Come on, Aunt May, where are...
...you?
Greetings, Spider-Man.
Why so wary?
You'll see there's nothing up my sleeve.
Except for my fist!
SMASH!
Close, but no cigar as they say.

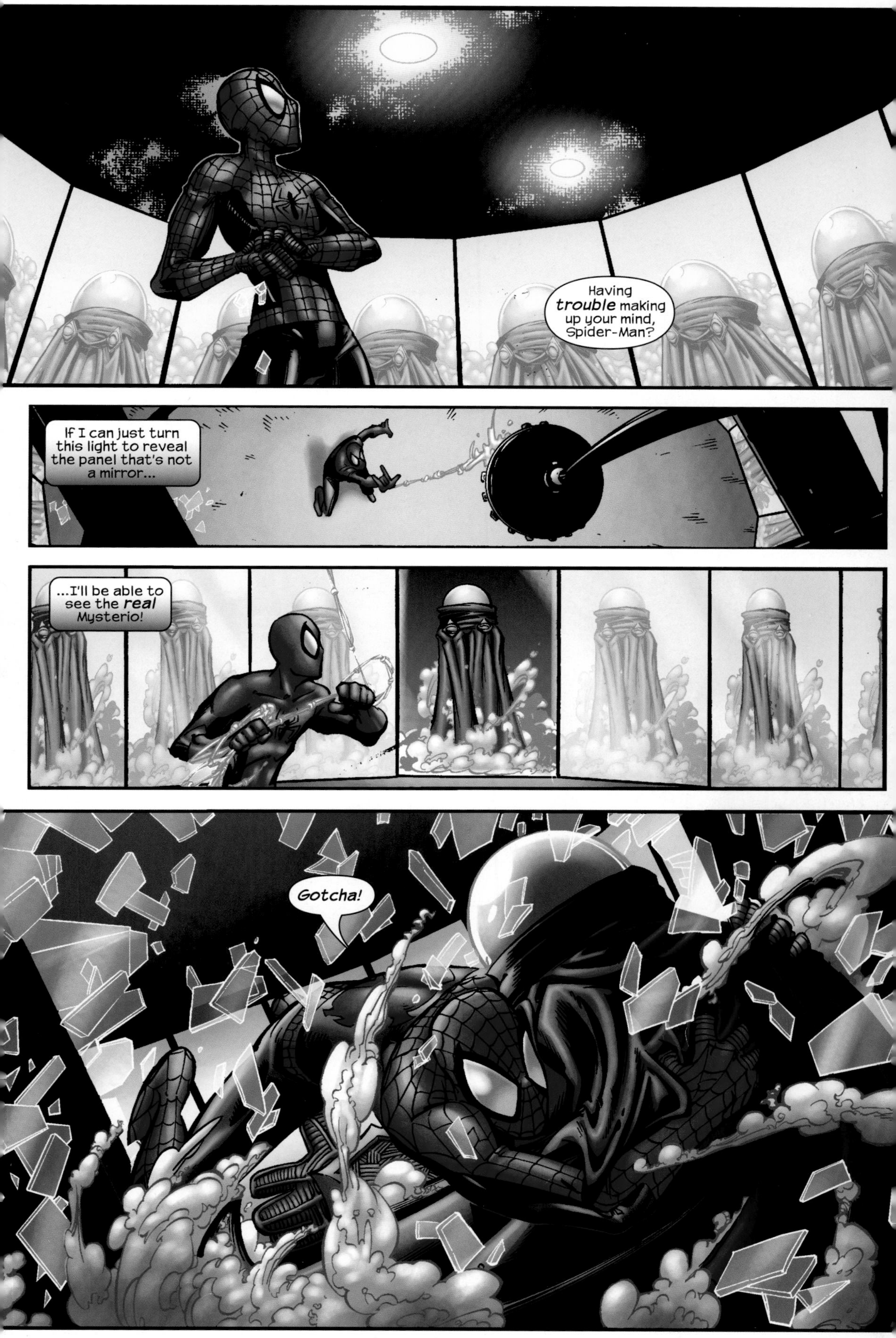
Having *trouble* making up your mind, Spider-Man?
If I can just turn this light to reveal the panel that's not a mirror...
...I'll be able to see the *real* Mysterio!
Gotcha!

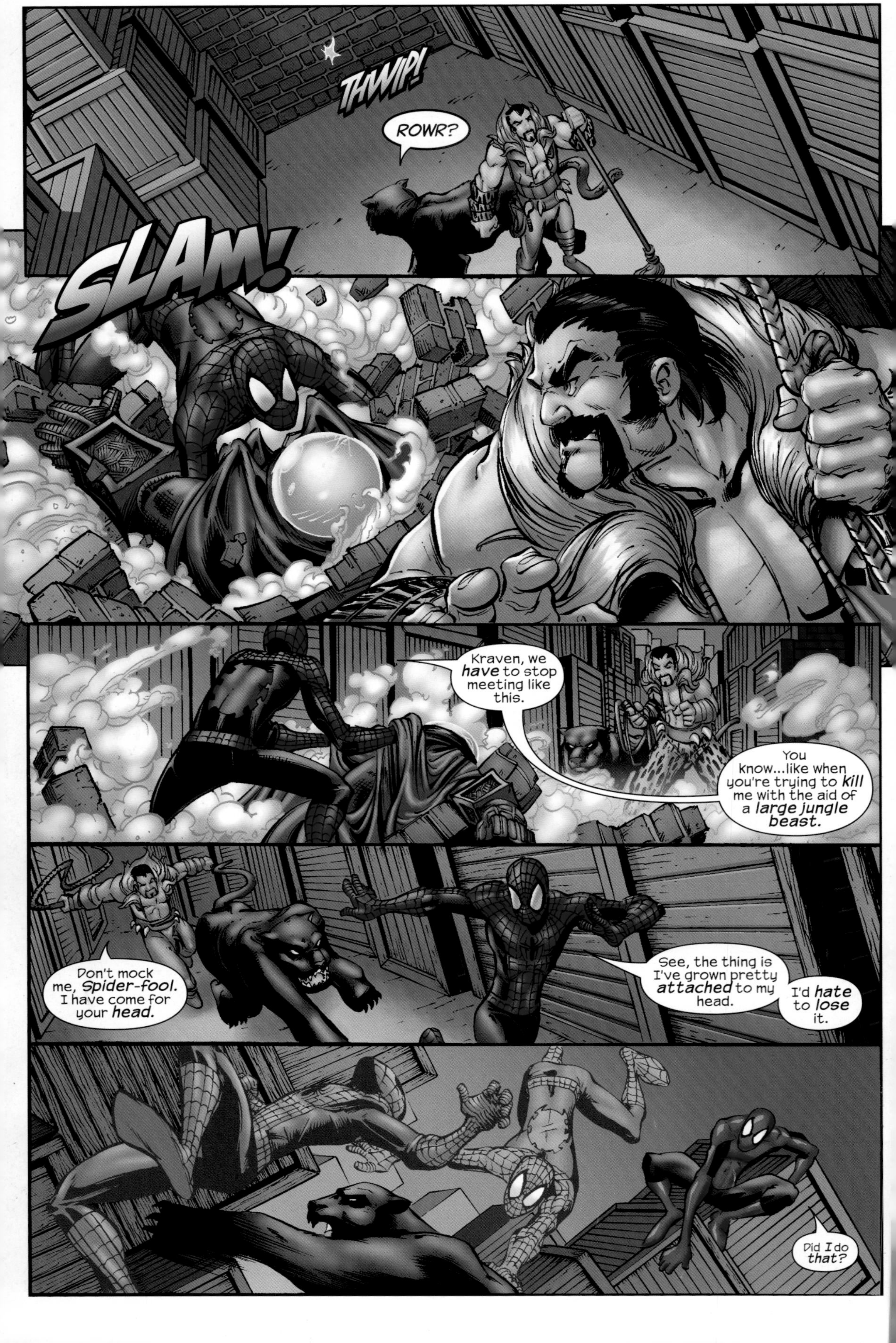
THWIP!
ROWR?
SLAM!
Kraven, we have to stop meeting like this.
You know...like when you're trying to kill me with the aid of a large jungle beast.
Don't mock me, Spider-fool. I have come for your head.
See, the thing is I've grown pretty attached to my head.
I'd hate to lose it.
Did I do that?

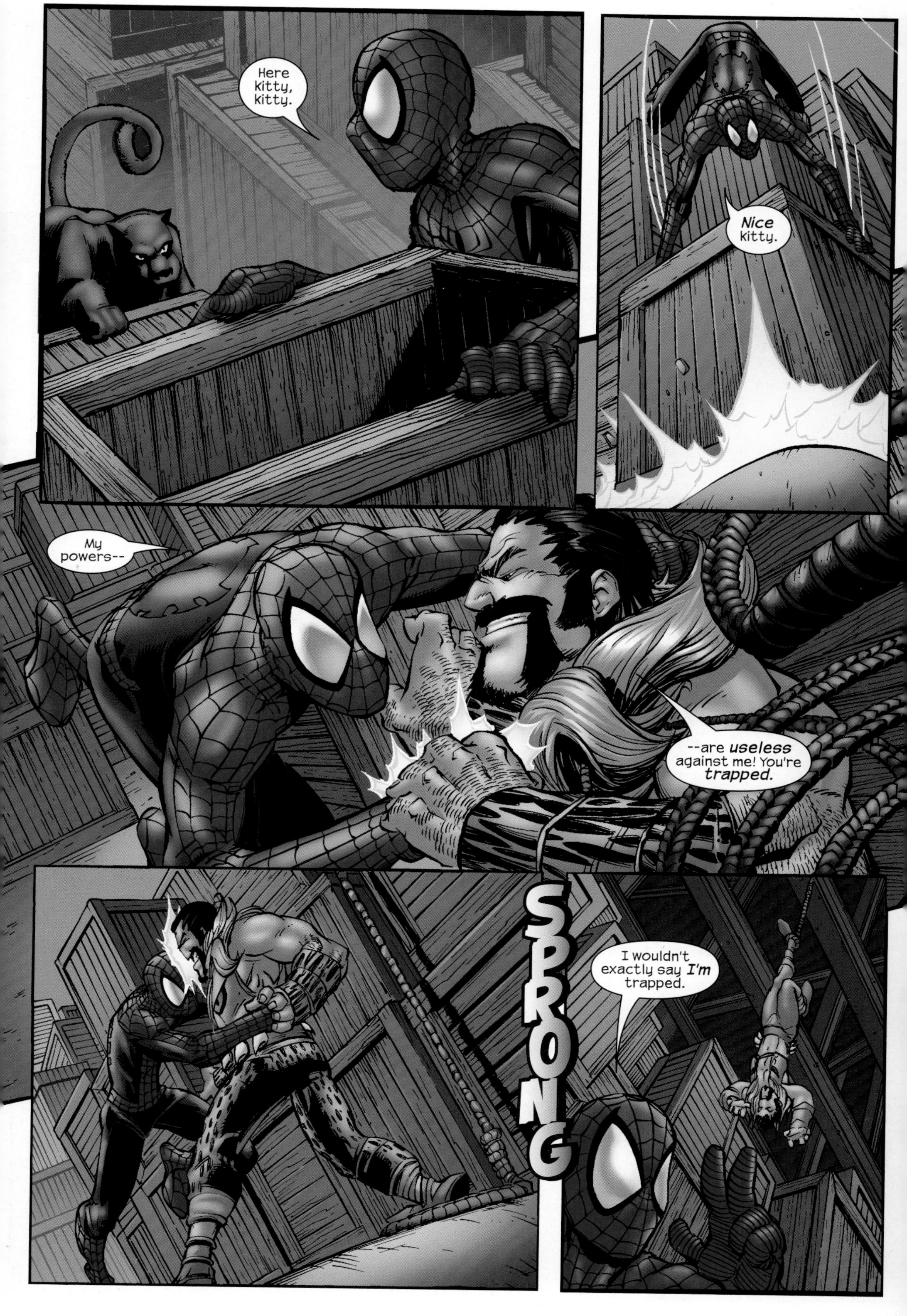
Here kitty, kitty.
Nice kitty.
My powers--
--are useless against me! You're trapped.
SPRONG
I wouldn't exactly say I'm trapped.

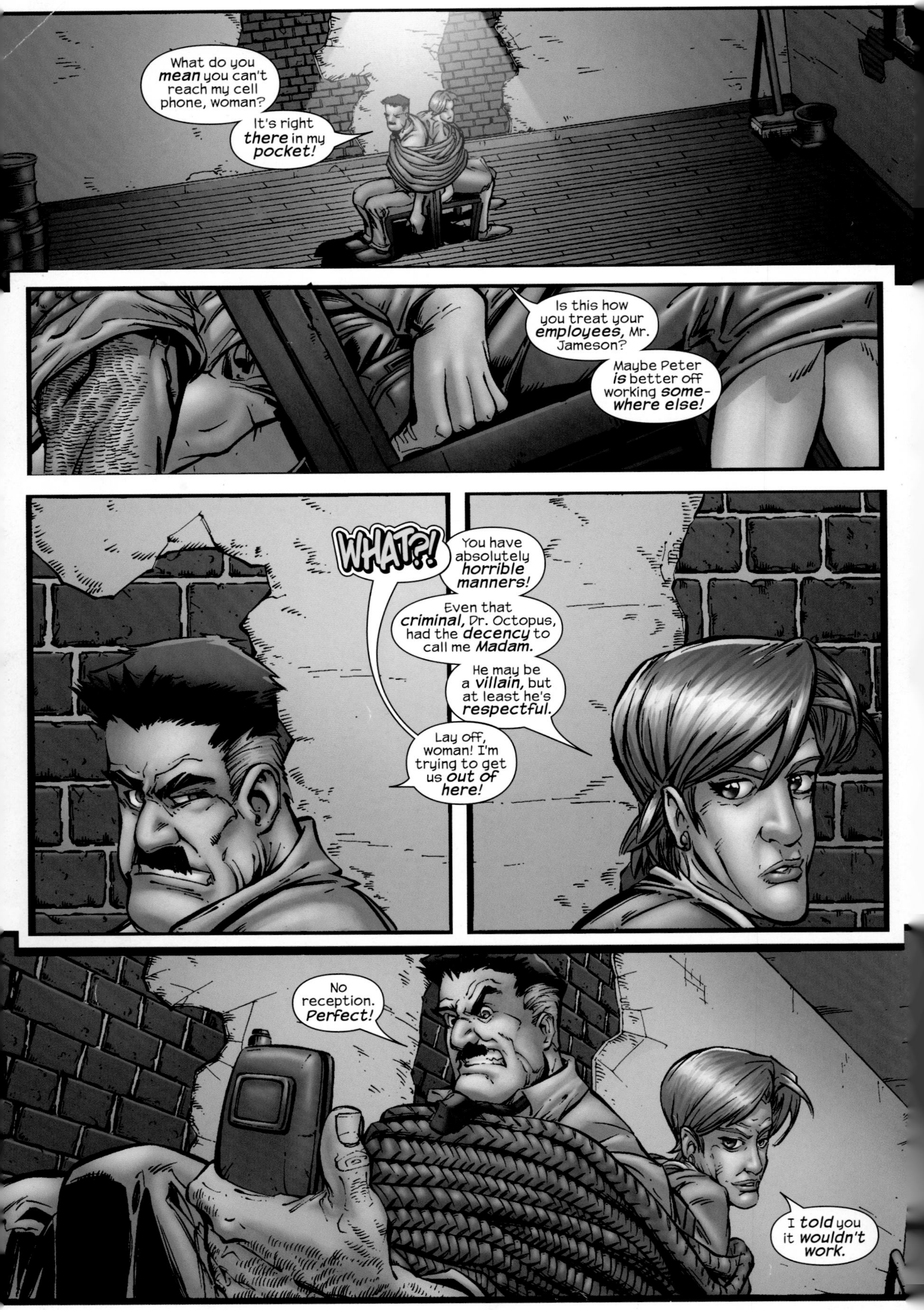

What do you mean you can't reach my cell phone, woman?
It's right there in my pocket!
Is this how you treat your employees, Mr. Jameson?
Maybe Peter is better off working some-where else!
WHAT?!
You have absolutely horrible manners!
Even that criminal, Dr. Octopus, had the decency to call me Madam.
He may be a villain, but at least he's respectful.
Lay off, woman! I'm trying to get us out of here!
No reception. Perfect!
I told you it wouldn't work.

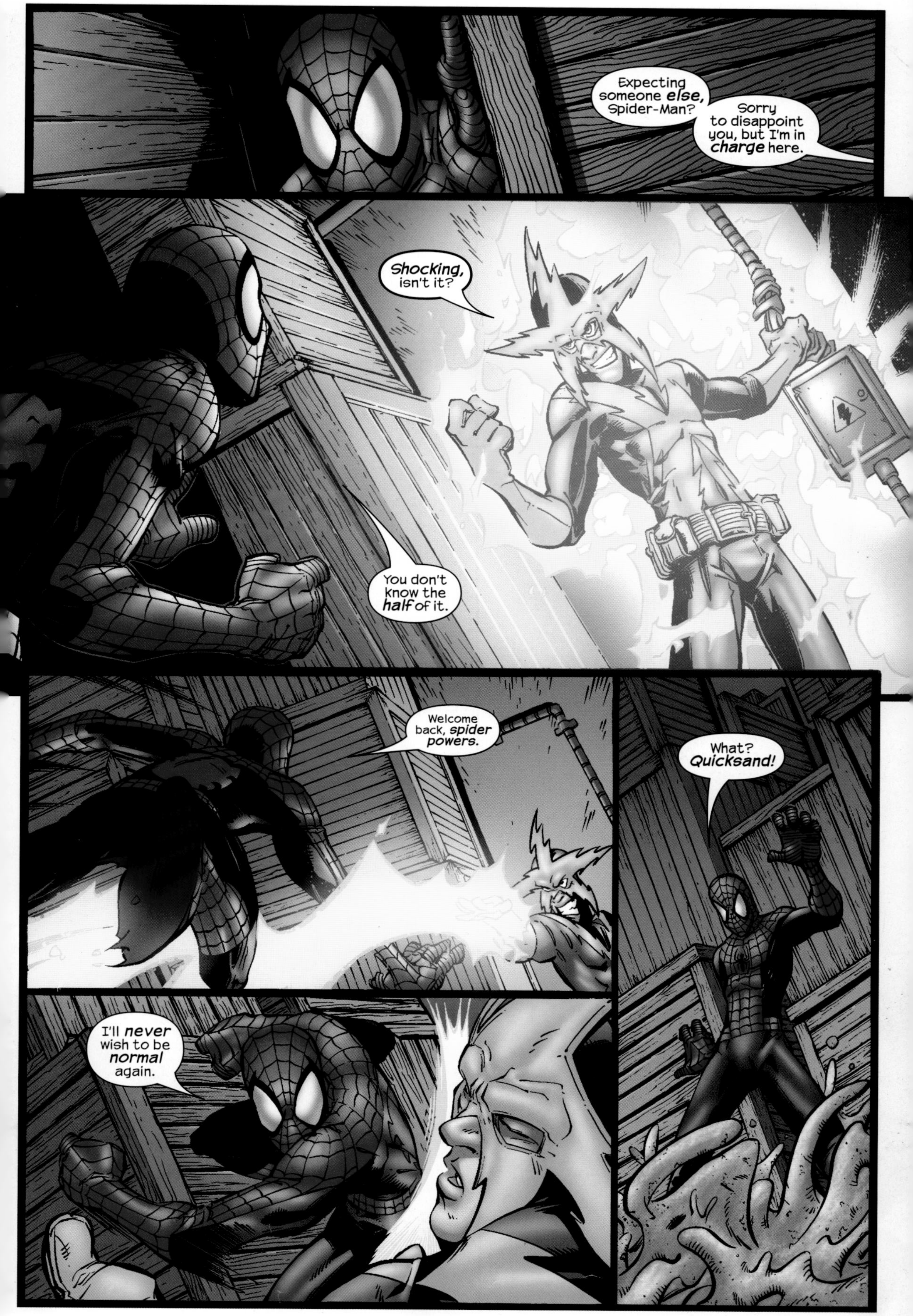
Expecting someone *else,* Spider-Man?
Sorry to disappoint you, but I'm in *charge* here.
Shocking, isn't it?
You don't know the *half* of it.
Welcome back, *spider powers.*
I'll *never* wish to be *normal* again.
What? *Quicksand!*

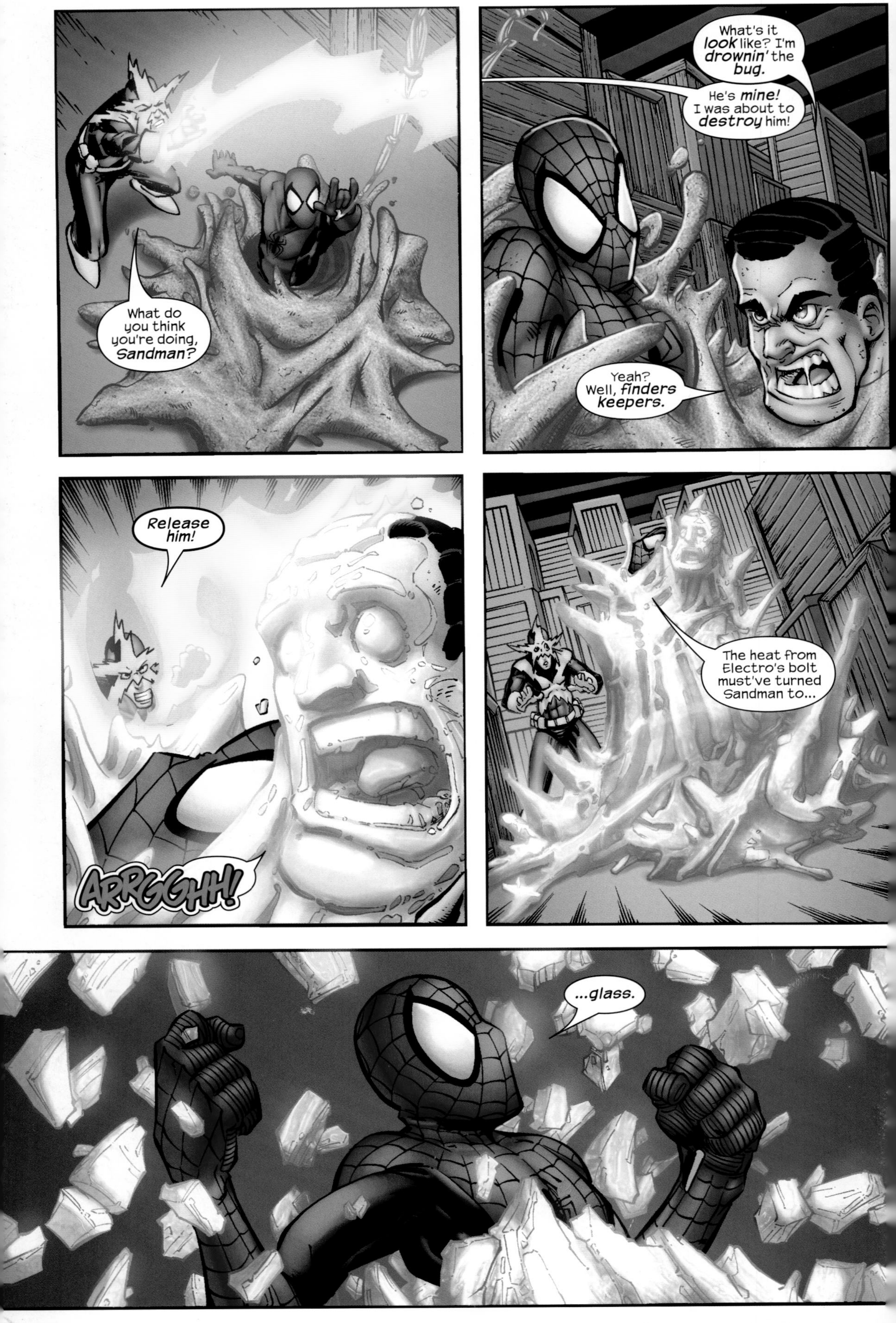
What do you think you're doing, Sandman?
What's it look like? I'm drownin' the bug.
He's mine! I was about to destroy him!
Yeah? Well, finders keepers.
Release him!
ARRGGHH!
The heat from Electro's bolt must've turned Sandman to...
...glass.

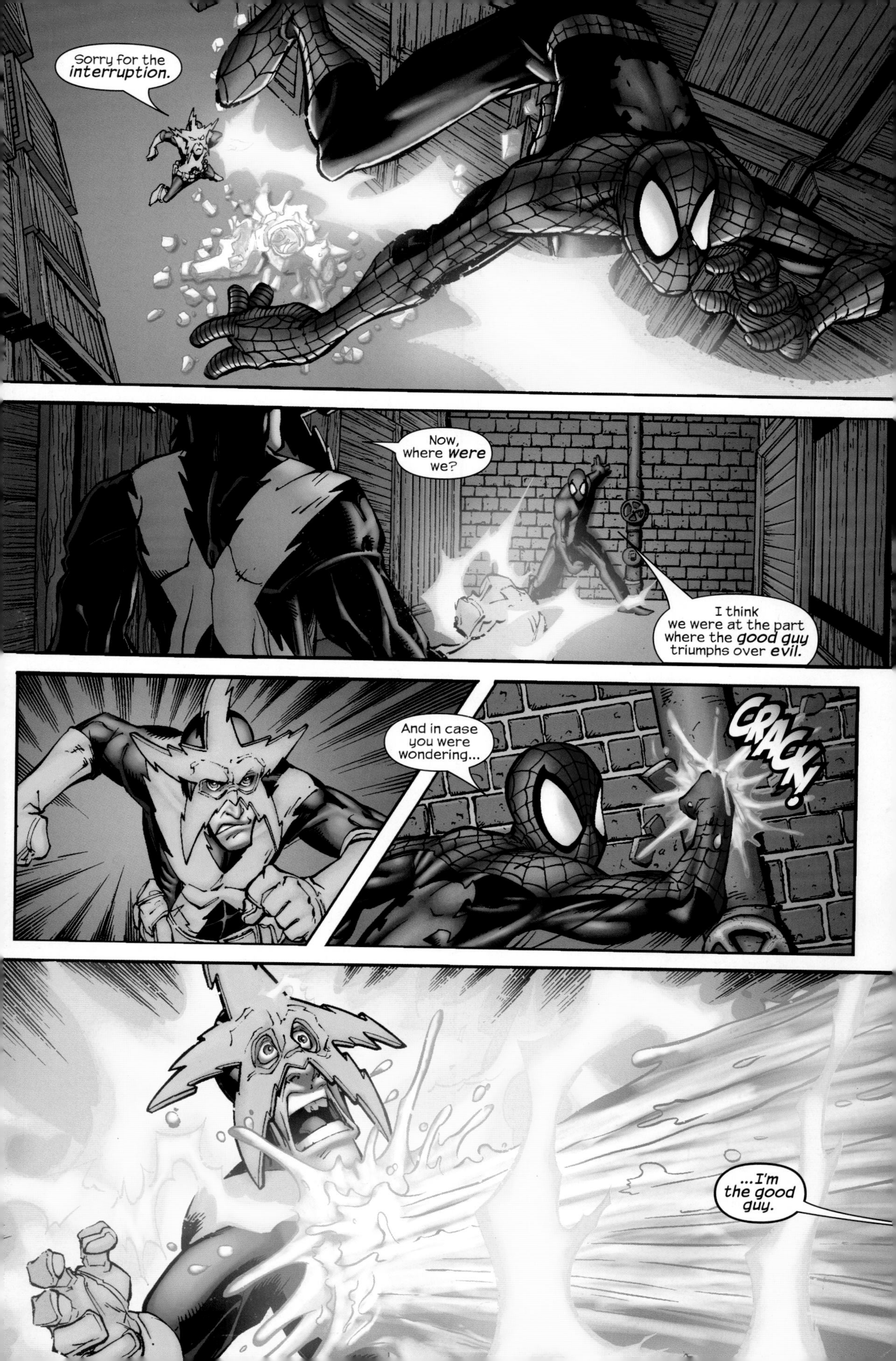
Sorry for the interruption.
Now, where were we?
I think we were at the part where the good guy triumphs over evil.
And in case you were wondering...
CRACK!
...I'm the good guy.

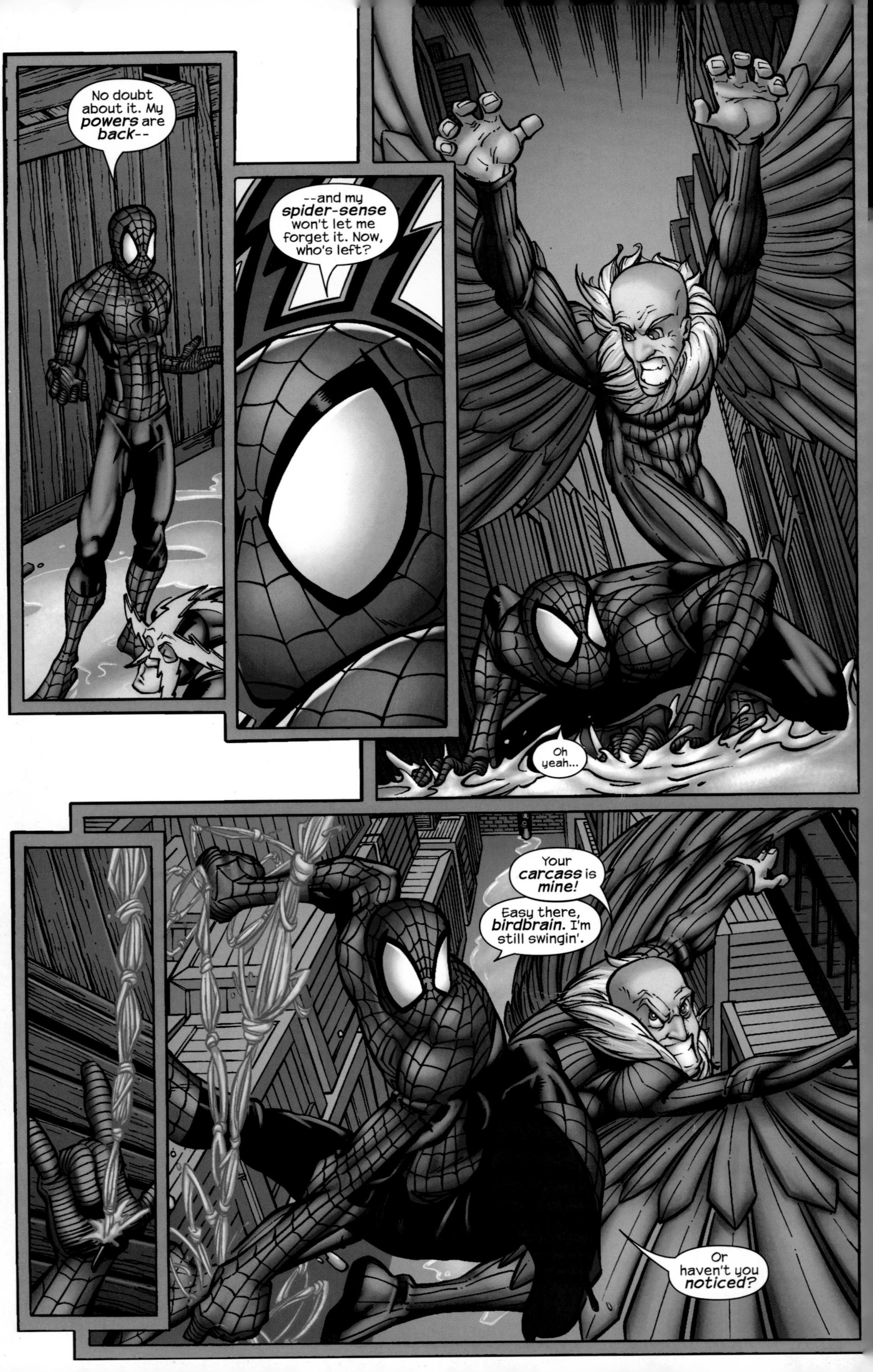
No doubt about it. My *powers* are *back*--
--and my *spider-sense* won't let me forget it. Now, who's left?
Oh yeah...
Your *carcass* is *mine!*
Easy there, ***birdbrain.*** I'm still swingin'.
Or haven't you *noticed?*

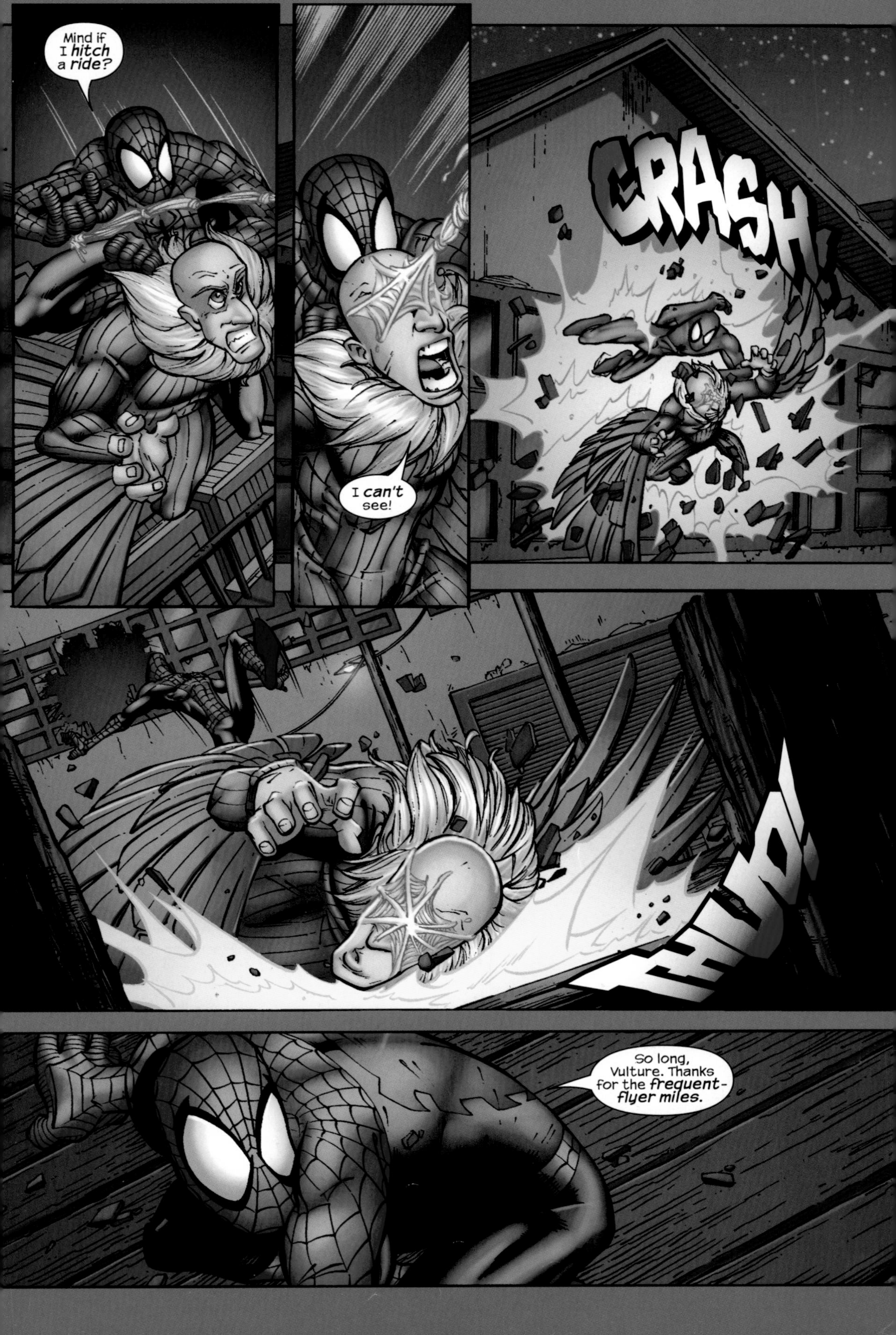
Mind if I *hitch* a *ride*?
I *can't* see!
CRASH!
So long, Vulture. Thanks for the *frequent-flyer miles*.

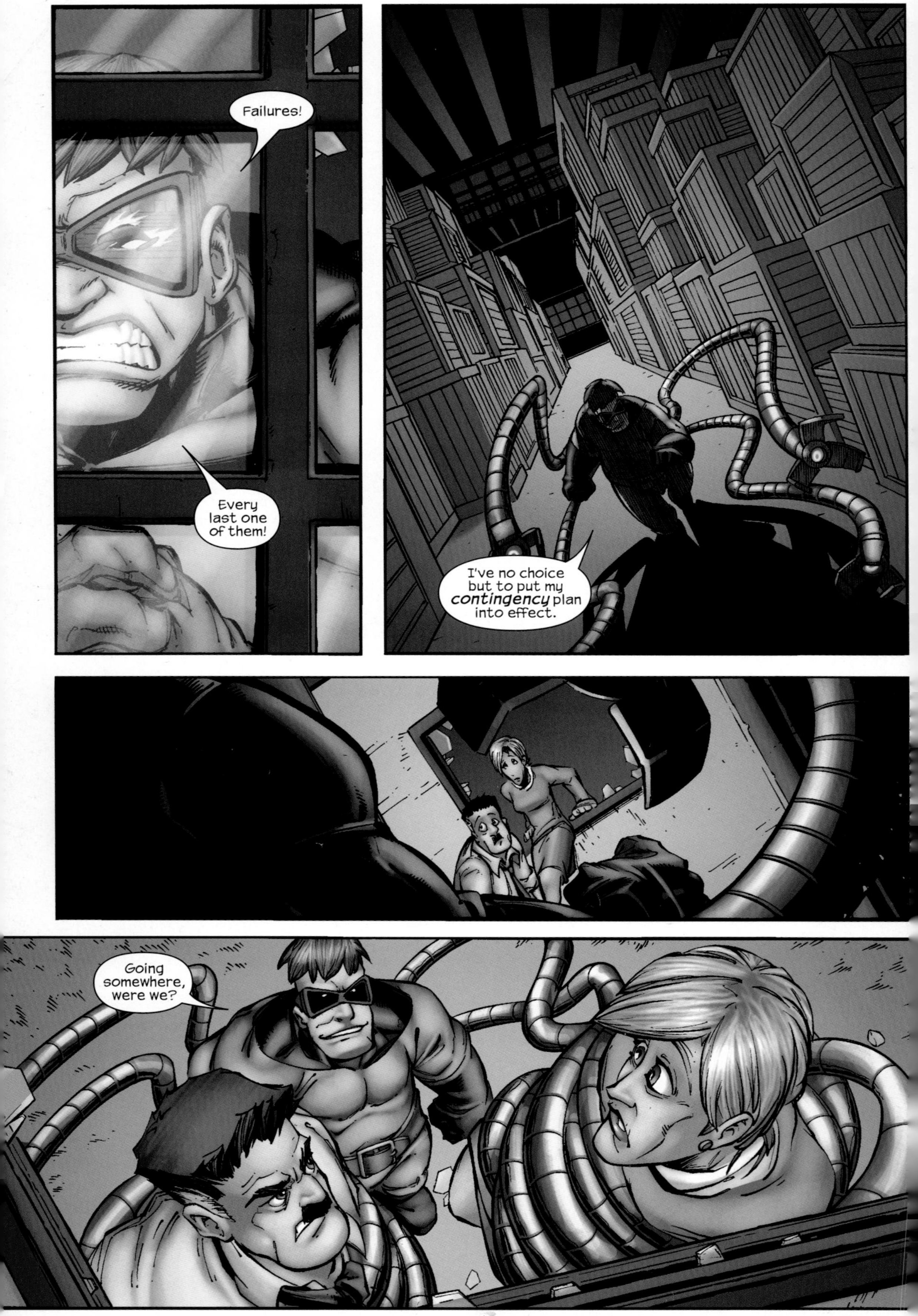
Failures!
Every last one of them!
I've no choice but to put my *contingency* plan into effect.
Going somewhere, were we?

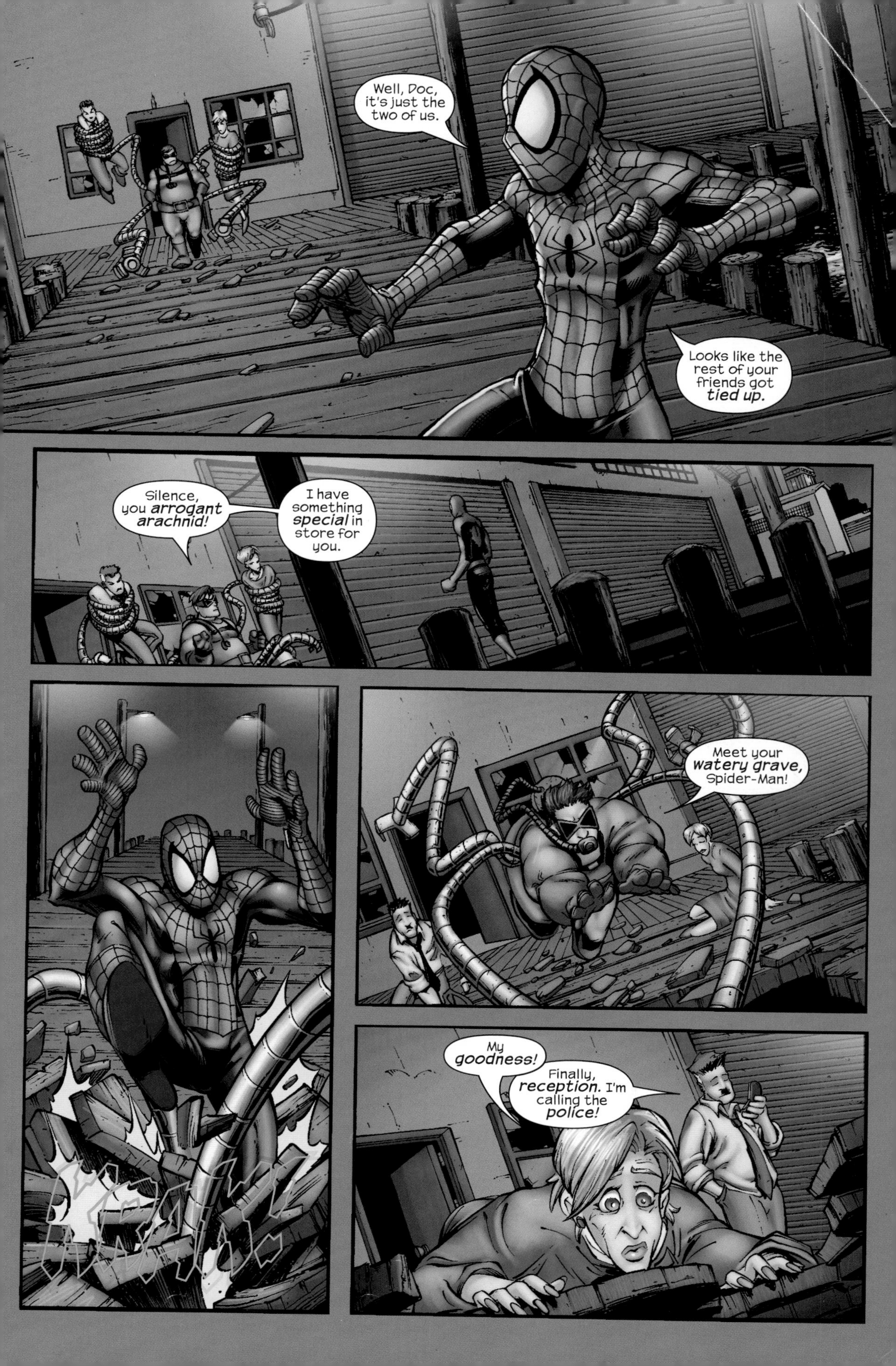
Well, Doc, it's just the two of us.
Looks like the rest of your friends got *tied up.*
Silence, you *arrogant arachnid!*
I have something *special* in store for you.
Meet your *watery grave,* Spider-Man!
My *goodness!*
Finally, *reception.* I'm calling the *police!*

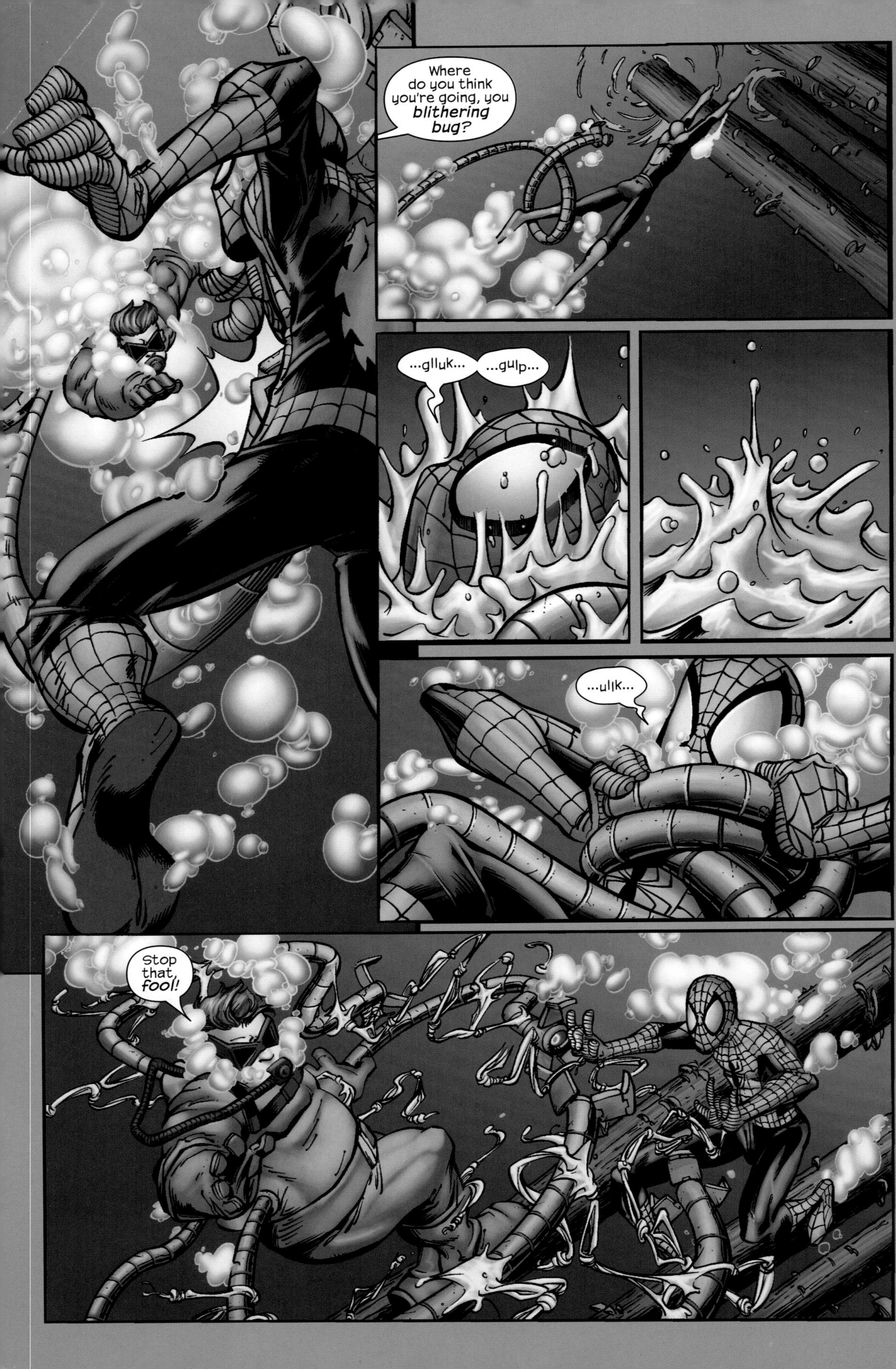
Where do you think you're going, you *blithering* *bug*?
...gllluk...
...gulp...
...ullk...
Stop that, *fool*!

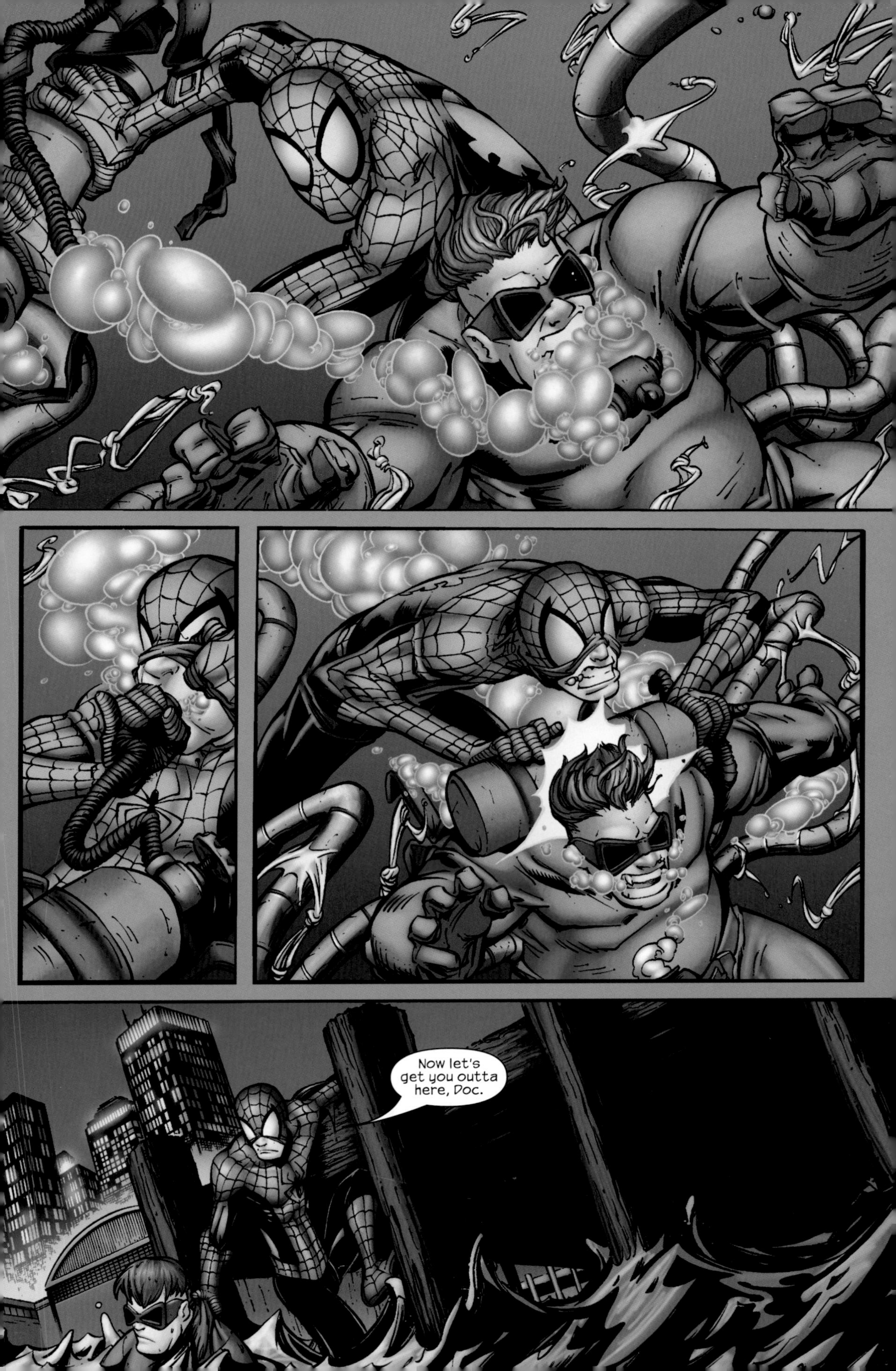
Now let's get you outta here, Doc.

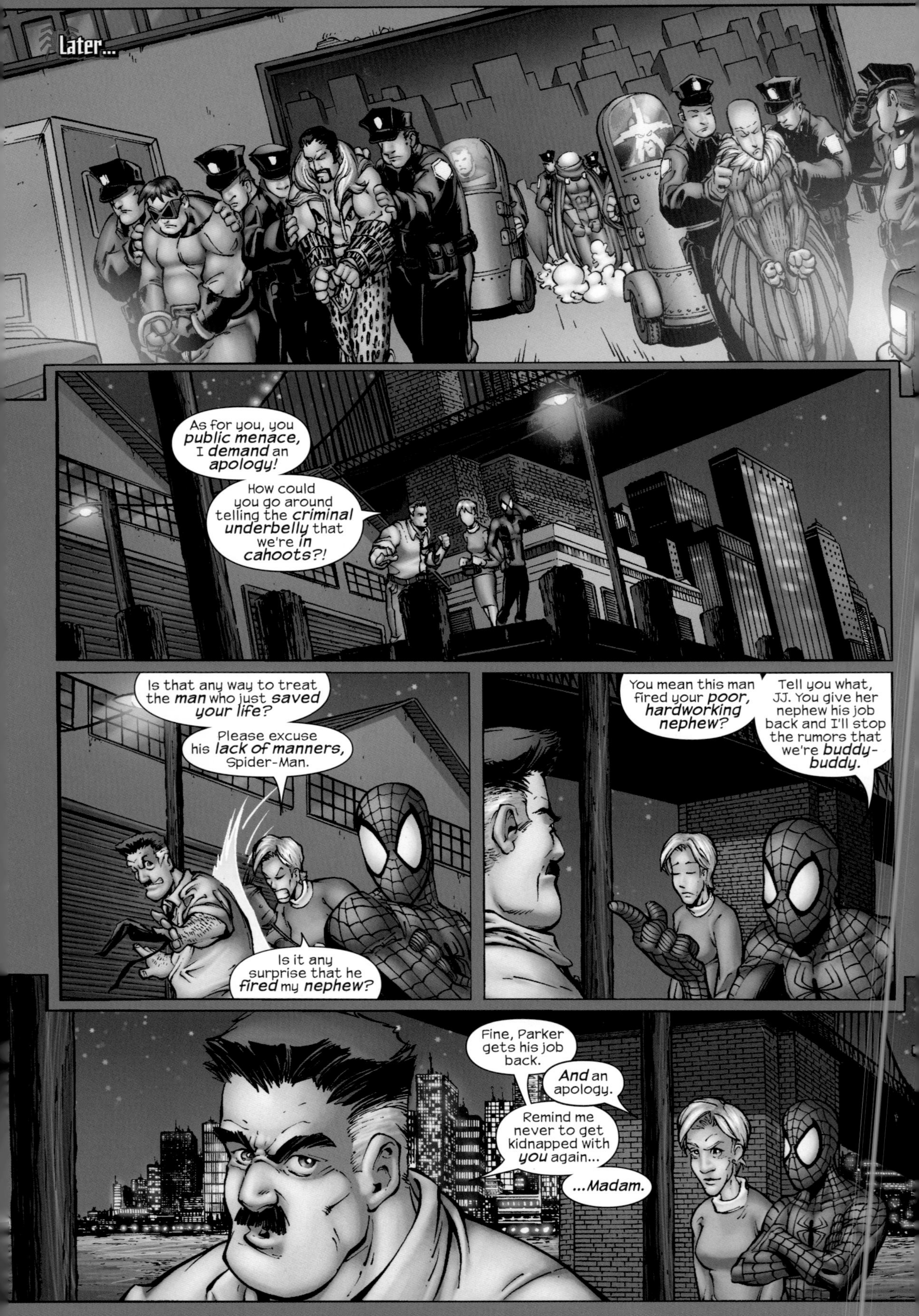
Later...
As for you, you public menace, I demand an apology!
How could you go around telling the criminal underbelly that we're in cahoots?!
Is that any way to treat the man who just saved your life?
Please excuse his lack of manners, Spider-Man.
Is it any surprise that he fired my nephew?
You mean this man fired your poor, hardworking nephew?
Tell you what, JJ. You give her nephew his job back and I'll stop the rumors that we're buddy-buddy.
Fine, Parker gets his job back.
And an apology.
Remind me never to get kidnapped with you again...
...Madam.

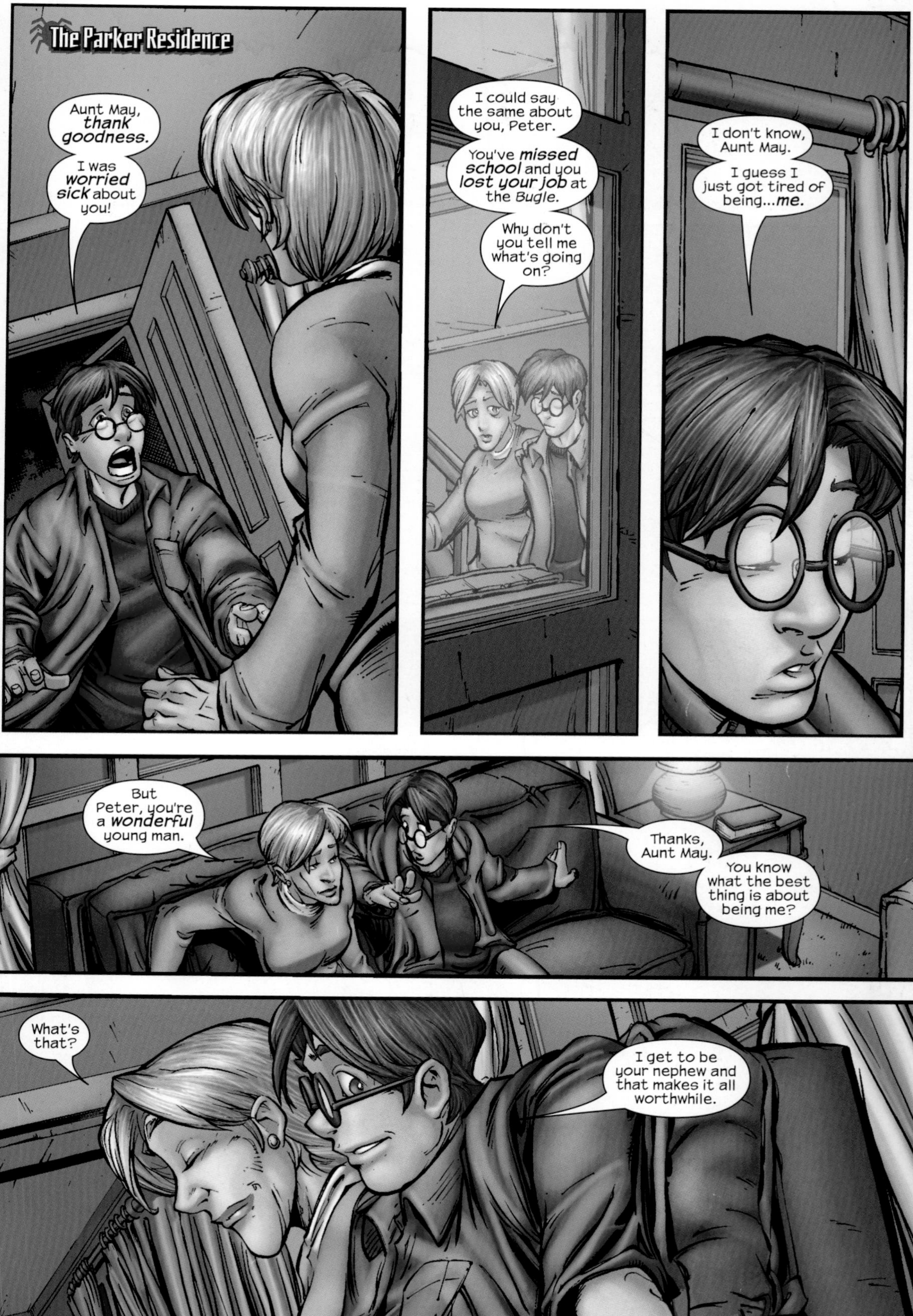
The Parker Residence
Aunt May, thank goodness.
I was worried sick about you!
I could say the same about you, Peter.
You've missed school and you lost your job at the Bugle.
Why don't you tell me what's going on?
I don't know, Aunt May.
I guess I just got tired of being...me.
But Peter, you're a wonderful young man.
Thanks, Aunt May.
You know what the best thing is about being me?
What's that?
I get to be your nephew and that makes it all worthwhile.

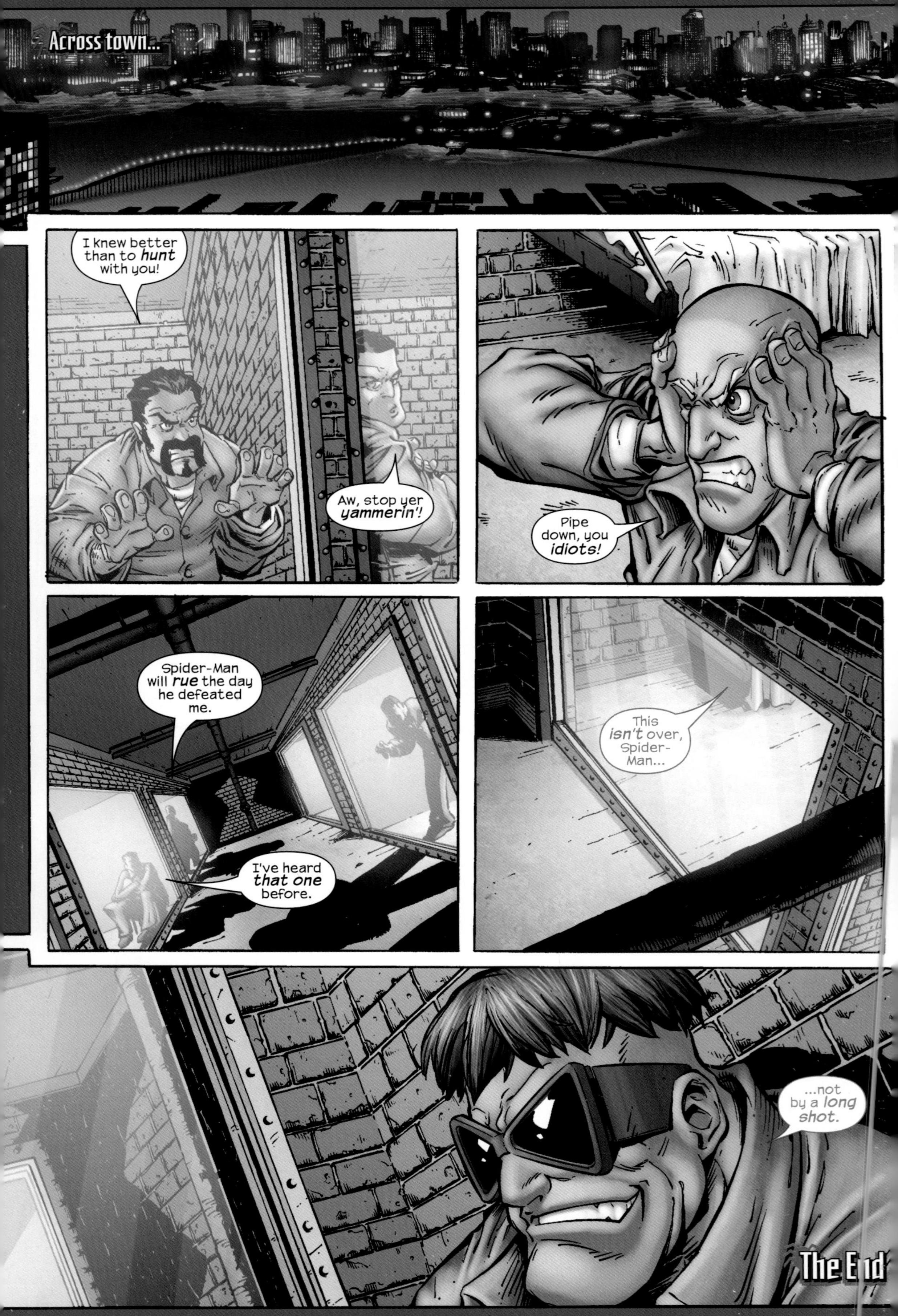
Across town...
I knew better than to *hunt* with you!
Aw, stop yer *yammerin'*!
Pipe down, you *idiots!*
Spider-Man will *rue* the day he defeated me.
I've heard *that one* before.
This *isn't* over, Spider-Man...
...not by a *long shot.*
The End